Teased

One Handed Reads
Book 1

Dee Lish

Chapter One

She stands in front of me, dressed in a sexy little feminine outfit that makes me wet almost instantly. Black heels over white stockings, which I know from experience means that she's also wearing white lace suspenders, bra, and knickers. She has a cute little black floral cotton skater dress over the top. Her makeup is perfect; long fake eyelashes, and ruby-red lips, which are currently greeting me with a seductive smirk. Her hair is in a cute little bob, just skimming her shoulders. Neat as always. My girl is, to me, walking perfection.

"You're wearing too many clothes," she remarks. "You know I like you naked when we're together."

I stand and begin to remove my clothing. I don't waste any time, pulling off my knickers with my leggings. My bra and top disappear soon after that. "Happy now?" I grin at her, holding my hands out to my sides, letting her enjoy every inch of my nude form.

"Come here," she demands and moves towards me, grabbing me at the back of my neck and pulling me tight against her. She cups my face in her hands, and my hands instinctively move around her waist. Quickly, her lips descend on mine, her tongue pushing into my mouth with force, demanding I accept.

I gladly take her tongue into my mouth, lapping at it with mine before sucking on it gently. A soft moan greets my actions and my fingers dig into her hips as my desire builds, increasing the wetness between my legs.

She lets one hand stray down over my bare skin as she kisses me. She cups a tit in her hand and rolls my nipple between her thumb and forefinger, making it my turn to moan against her mouth.

Her hand strays further, skimming over my hips and stomach before reaching its ultimate goal between my legs. She pushes her finger between my labia, my arousal ensuring she meets no resistance before her digit grazes my clit. I groan, my hips involuntarily pushing back against her hand.

"Always ready for me, aren't you?" she breathes against my lips as she breaks our kiss. "You're such a whore."

I know name-calling probably shouldn't turn me on, but it does.

She lifts her hand away from my pussy and rubs her fingers over my lips. Instinctively, I run my tongue over the wet trail she leaves, and she seizes the opportunity to direct me to suck her fingers clean of my pussy juices.

Tasting myself on her fingers just increases my need. I suck on them hungrily, and she laughs. "Good girl. You clean my fingers. Suck them like you will my cock."

My pulse quickens at the thought of her using her strap-on with me, but before I get the chance to think about it too hard, she puts her hand on my shoulder and pushes me. I drop to my knees and she puts her foot forward in my direction.

"Kiss it," she demands, and I sink to my hands and knees and lean forward to kiss her foot. I know she's not about the dominance of the act. My girl just likes to perv on my arse in the air while I kiss her feet. I give it a peck and look up at her.

"You can do better than that," she says, and I run my tongue over her shoe and the top of her foot in long, lavish strokes.

"Good girl." She grins down at me, knowing full well what effect calling me that has on me. When she's satisfied that I've paid enough attention to both feet, she tells me to turn from her, touch my nose to the floor, and keep my arse up in the air.

I eagerly await what she's going to do to me next when I feel a cold dribble of lubricant run over my asshole. Just enough not to cause damage, but definitely not enough to be anything but painfully aware of what she's doing.

The tip of something is pressed against my asshole, and I wait as she slides the butt plug deep inside without too much concern for my comfort. She gives me a good, hard smack on the arse, making sure to slap the base of the plug in the process. She strokes over my arse and slips her fingers back between my legs, teasing my clit again, making me move against her hand. I want to come, already so full of need. Just before I get to that point, she pulls her hand away, and I groan in frustration.

"Get on the bed, on your back, and lean your head right on the edge," she tells me.

I do as I'm told. She turns to face away from me, then backs towards me and straddles my head. She lowers herself to my face before covering me with her lace-covered cunt.

"Lick me," she demands.

I move my tongue against her knickers, seeking out her

cunt and working my mouth against her, teasing her, making sure I have her just as aroused as she has me.

I hook my tongue past her knickers, making contact with her skin, and lick along her now exposed cunt, running my tongue around her entrance before fucking into her. She grinds against my face and moans her satisfaction. I grab her thighs with my hands and keep her pulled tight against my face. I can barely breathe and it makes me dizzy, but that only turns me on even more. I need to make her come so badly, and she knows it.

She breaks our contact and stand, then turns to face me. "Drop your head back off the bed a little more."

I do as I'm told. Once there, I'm greeted with a full view of what she has in mind for me. Knowing I'm watching her every move, she lifts her dress slowly and pulls down the front of her knickers, revealing the big, hard strap-on she had tucked away this whole time.

"Hands over your head," she tells me and straddles my head and arms. "Open your mouth."

When I do, she dips her hips, slips the head of her cock between my lips, and then leans over the length of my body, supporting her weight on either side of my legs.

I know what's coming, and between this and the burning stretch my arse has had, I'm on fire, my cunt is slick, and all I want is what she has to give me.

She starts to thrust gentle little strokes into my mouth, allowing me the time to build up my greed. I lie there, a gloriously sexy stocking-covered thigh against each arm on either side of my face, and her cock getting deeper and deeper with each slow, teasing thrust. I'm greedy for her, though. I need more and push my face up towards her with each movement from her hips. She stops and withdraws completely so she can look down at me.

"You want it all?" she asks, and I nod. She looks down at me, lifts her dress again, and watches as she slowly slides her cock into my mouth.

I breathe through my nose and try to keep relaxed as she hits the back of my throat and stops, the balls of her strap-on resting against my nose.

"Jesus," she says breathlessly, looking down at me with all of her cock in my mouth. My gag reflex kicks in and she pulls out again. She quickly leans back over me and starts a fiercer fucking of my face, brutally thrusting into my mouth like she would my cunt, filling me with her cock.

She leans on me, her hand between my legs. I spread them to allow her access, and she sinks two fingers deep into my sopping cunt. I moan around her dick and move my arms to grab at her ass and pull her harder into my throat. The more I take in my mouth, the more she plays with my cunt until I can't take it anymore, and I scream out in climax with her dick firmly between my lips.

She pulls the strap-on from my mouth and slaps my tits.

"Get on your knees," she demands.

I move slowly, still basking in the post-orgasmic bliss. and get on all fours. She climbs onto the bed behind me and shoves my face to the mattress. "Ass up, good girl," she teases.

I feel her hands on the butt plug, and she pulls it from my ass, dropping it to the floor. Quickly, she takes her cock and pushes it against my arsehole before pushing it hard into me. I cry out as she stretches my arse out with her dick, pushing it into me until she's balls deep in my poor little arse. My cunt throbs with need, and I groan and start to shift against her.

I can't help but think of how this must look, me completely naked, while she's still dressed perfectly, taking me hard in my greedy arse with a big fat cock. She pounds my ass without mercy until the need to come again rises in me. She spanks me hard as she pounds into me, and I come apart with her buried deep in my arse. I scream out, pushing back against her, needing to feel every last inch of her dick inside me. Then I feel it; her cock empties into me, filling me with cum. My hips give way, and she collapses on top of me, both of us panting, her cock still firmly inside me.

I know my place. Naked and at the ruthless mercy of my girl.

Chapter Two

I love stretching out in the passenger side of his black BMW 3 Series. There's just something about being in his company that I find utterly intoxicating. From the second I'm in the same space as him, a calmness falls over me. The knowledge that, in that moment, I'm exactly where I should be. Maybe it's the extent of my feelings for him or just his strong, manly presence. Something about his broad shoulders and tall stature that generate that flush of serenity. Whatever it is, at those times, I am content to be nowhere else in the world.

Miles pass, idle chitchat fades, and his closeness takes over. My pussy gets wetter, my nipples stiffen, and my breasts ache to be in his firm grip. But we have a long drive ahead of us, and it's going to be a while before that will be possible.

More miles sail past outside and the atmosphere inside the car is slowly charging with sexual electricity. I feel his eyes keep scanning over me, and I glance at him.

"All right?" he asks before returning his eyes to the road.

"Yeah, I'm all good," I reply. "I just need to be naked with you, and sooner rather than later."

That delicious smirk he has flashes across his mouth, and a sly sideways glance is shot in my direction.

"Good." He grins.

"Not good," I reply. "I'm already wet and horny."

Another look is shot in my direction. "You can wait," he tells me with more of a smirk.

I return it with a cheeky look on my face. "I don't really have to," I tell him. "I'm not the one driving." I reach for the seat controls, leaning back, getting myself some more space while still wearing my seatbelt.

My hands cup my breasts and give them a small squeeze. His eyes flick over to me and back to the road. "Keep driving, mister," I warn him, and slide my hands up underneath my top.

"Stop distracting me, then. It's dangerous!"

My hands roam over my tits under my clothes. My nipples pebble, and I can't resist the temptation of pulling on my bra and letting my breasts pop out, so I can get more access to my aching tits.

"Jesus," he says from the driver's seat.

"Keep your eyes on the road," I tell him, a sexual sigh following as I roll my nipples between my thumb and forefinger.

"Jen, if we have an accident, it's all your fault," he growls as he shifts uncomfortably in his seat. I can tell by how he moves that he's already hard for me. *Good. Let him suffer a little.*

My fingers vary between rolling my nipples with my thumb and grazing them with my fingertips, circling them, letting my nerve endings sizzle, my pussy getting wetter. Soft sighs and moans bubble up within me.

"Fuck," comes the curse of frustration from beside me.

"Mmmm," I hum breathlessly.

"Don't do it," he warns.

"I can't. Only you make me come with just my nipples being played with. For that, I need to do this…" I slide a hand into my leggings and slip it under my knickers, finding my pussy swollen and soaked.

I waste no time in spreading my legs as best I can in the front of his car and seeking out my clit.

"Mmmm, fuck," I hiss when my fingertip first caresses that sensitive little bundle of nerves.

"Christ," he groans beside me. "You're making it practically impossible to concentrate on the road."

I couldn't reply even if I wanted to. I'm already too focussed on the circling motion as I run my fingers over my clit, tempting and teasing myself onwards to the inevitable.

My heart speeds and my breathing gets quicker and shallower, my hand moves faster, and I know his eyes are boring holes into me. That knowledge makes my skin prickle with excitement, heightening the sensation that's building in my pussy.

I can feel my climax coming from the thrill of being in the car as it travels along where anyone from a higher vehicle can see what I'm doing. I know he's looking at me more than the road. I know this will be in his mind anytime he thinks of me in the car now too.

Before I know it, a powerful orgasm slams into me. I cry out loudly. Every muscle in my body tenses and colours decorate the backs of my closed eyelids. He pulls my hand from my leggings, and when my eyes finally open, he's putting my soaked fingertips into his mouth.

"Fuck," he sighs, as he lets his tongue trace over my fingers, tasting my juices. "You're going to pay for this later."

His voice is laced with lust. "I think my dirty girl needs a good spanking." He sucks on my index finger. "But first I'm going to fuck you the second we get to the hotel. You need it. Hard."

My pussy clenches and soaks even more.

As usual, I tease him, and he ends up being the one to drive me even more crazy. I should learn this each time, but I think that might be the real thrill in this little car sexcapade. No matter how much I tease him, he will always come back with the upper hand. And that's just how I like it.

Chapter Three

I finally make it out of the airport. He gets out of the car when he sees me, and when I get to him, he pulls me close against him for a hug. I revel in that contact, his arms around me, holding me tight.

"Hello, you," I breathe out against his ear. His lips meet mine, and I melt in against him, welcoming his tongue with mine. It's all I need to tell him in that moment. *Hello. I've missed you. I can't wait to have you alone.* Once our hellos have been said sufficiently, he grabs my case and throws it into the boot before we each head for our own side of his car. We pass the time with the usual idle chitchat. How was the flight? How's work? Until we're finally out on a main road and heading away from the airport.

When he leaves his hand resting on the gear stick, I take the opportunity to put my hand over it and guide it between my legs. I make sure to grind his hand in against what I'm trying to show him.

"Do you feel that?" I grin. He glances over at me and I know that look on his face all too well.

A small, cheeky smirk flashes across his lips. "I think you know what's going to happen to you once we've checked in."

I smirk back and let him think about what's going to happen for the rest of the short journey to the hotel. I watch the scenery pass by and flick through the music on his stereo.

I grab my case from the boot and make my way to reception to talk nicely to the man arranging my room key. Since he's standing beside me, I let my hand drop from the counter as I tap in my debit card PIN with the other hand. I let it rest against his crotch before applying a little pressure and rubbing against his cock that's trapped behind his jeans. I smile sweetly at the clerk, releasing my hand from him and taking the room key with it. I turn and head to the lift, letting him follow.

Nothing else is said until we get to the room. I dump my case and move back towards him. I push him hard against the wall and, again, my hand goes to his cock. My other hand grabs his and places it firmly over my strap-on. I rub over his length.

"I'm going to have this later. But first..." I pause, making him rub my own length, "...you're going to have this." I grin.

Hooded lids cover lust-filled eyes as his mouth descends on mine again. His arousal at the whole idea is oh-so-very apparent.

He kisses me hard, and again, my body moulds against his, responding to him in every way possible. I pull back from him and lead him by the hand, steering him over to the other side of the bed on the opposite side of the room. I circle him, running my hands leisurely over him through his t-shirt. Once at his rear, I pull one hand behind his back and guide it down to my strap-on. I encourage him to rub me, letting him stroke me like he would if it was a real dick. While he's enjoying that feeling, I slip my hand over his cock and rub it hard.

I grab his other hand and repeat the action, letting both of his hands roam over my strap-on, making friends with my cock before I make him intimately acquainted with it. I wrap my arms around him and pull his back against my front, my hands slipping under his t-shirt and running my fingers over his stomach and up over his chest. My fingertips focus on their goal of his nipples, and I graze them with my nails.

"I'm going to give you my cock, and there's not a damn thing you can do to stop me, is there?" I tease him.

A moan rumbles in his chest, and his fingers flex against my cock. "I guess not."

I run my hands back down over his skin, towards his waistband. I undo the button on the top of his jeans and glide the zip down. I push his legs apart with my foot and let his jeans slide to the floor. I follow them, making sure they are pooled at his ankles. As I rise back up, I run my hands over the outside of his legs before running them over his crotch when I stand up straight again.

His hard dick bobs in my hand in response to my touch. "Awww, you're so hard for a man who is about to get taken hard up the arse," I tease against his back.

"Oh, fuck!"

I grab the waistband of his boxers and pull them down to join his jeans. I repeat the action of running my hands up over his legs, only this time, when I finally stand up, I run my hands over his arse and let my finger slip along the valley between his buttocks.

I push him hard, and he falls face-first to the bed, bending at the waist to try to stop his feet from leaving the floor. When he does, it just allows me more access to his arse, and I don't stop pushing until he's resting against the top of the bed. I pull the lube from my jeans pocket and spread it over my fingers, then slip it back into my pocket and return my now lubed-up hand to his ass crack.

"Spread your damn legs, whore," I bark at him. "I can't exactly make you my little bitch if you aren't going to spread your legs for me." I smack my other hand down hard on his bare buttock, and he opens his legs wider.

I rub my fingers over his semi-exposed asshole, pushing against it, needing to be inside him already. I feel him attempting to relax around my first two fingers as I penetrate his slutty, tight little arse. He feels amazing around my digits, and I let them slip in and out of him, stretching him, lubing him up, ready for my dick. He moans again and pushes back against me, and I can't resist slipping a third digit into his arse.

The experience is making me wet as hell. The sounds he's making, the way his arse rises to meet every thrust of my fingers, the delicious tightness of him, and how amazingly filthy he likes to be is a heady combination that has me longing for more. I need to both sink my cock into him and have him sink his cock into me. Plenty of time for that later, though. For now, I'm thoroughly turned on by having him take my fingers into him.

The temptation is just too much, and when I let my fingers slide from his ass this time, I move slightly to the side of him so he can see me as he's bent over the bed. I lift my fingers to my lips and suck on every lubed-up one of them. He sucks in air as he watches me.

"I couldn't resist licking my fingers. I needed to taste

you," I say with a smirk, and the moan he breathes out tells me all I need to know.

I move back in behind him, placing a hand on each buttock and pulling them apart before I bury my face between them, my tongue seeking out his ass. I lick my way around that tight little ring of muscle before pushing my tongue into him, teasing him, encouraging more amazing noises from him, and I rim and tongue fuck his delicious arse.

I grab his buttocks harder, my nails biting into his flesh, needing more of him as I grind my face and tongue against his ass and tight little hole. I relish in the feel of him against me, delighting in the appreciative sounds and sighs he's letting out, feeling the slickness of my pussy against my thighs, knowing it's not enough. I need to have my cock buried inside him so I can feel the base of it pressing against my clit with every thrust into him I give.

My tongue trails up the entire length of his ass crack, and I move back with a short sharp crack of my right hand against his buttock. I pull the lube out of my jeans pocket again before making fast work of pulling my jeans and the boxers that I bought to wear while I had my cock on to the floor. Stroking my faux cock in my hand, I flip the lid on the lube and rub it over my length. I squirt a substantial amount on the head of my dick and let a sizable drop trickle down to his arsehole.

I push forward, holding my cock at his ass, pushing the head in firmly.

He lets out a long groan as his ass takes me inside. "Oh, fuck, yes," he pants, and I begin slow, shallow thrusts, each time teasing in a little deeper.

I keep up the pace, needing to be deeper inside him, not stopping until my false balls touch him. Once he has me deep, I take even more delight in pulling out and slamming back into him. He groans with every stroke, his ass rising to meet me, pushing back on my length, needing it just as much as I do.

"You like that, don't you?" I tease him. When he doesn't reply, I slam into him, making him grunt sexually. "I can't hear you, bitch. What did you say?"

"Jesus, YES!" he breathes.

I grab his hips and drive into him harder. I need to make sure he knows just who owns his ass; to make sure he's left with the feeling that I've been deep inside him for days afterwards. The pressure on my clit with every thrust just keeps driving me on. My own climax starts to build, and I'm craving it more than anything right now. I pound his arse furiously, needing to come.

"Fuck, your ass feels so good. God, you're such a whore, taking my dick so well. You're just such a fucking slut!" I taunt him again. "Tell me what you are!" I spank my hand down on his right buttock.

"Ohhh, fuck," he moans. "I'm your slut."

"Whose slut?" I ask, grinding against him while fully embedded up his arse.

A sharp exhale of breath makes me grin, and he moans, "Yours. Oh, fuck. I'm your whore!" I grin at his reply and sigh, my head falling back and my eyes closing as I savour every delicious feeling this is generating in me.

His moans of lust grow louder. He's pushing back on me with every stroke. My own sighs of pleasure start to mix with his, and I just can't help but keep driving on. Everything becomes one long sound of ass fucking between us. His groans, my moans, and the sound of my body slapping against his ass as I slam into him again and again. The pressure builds inside me, and heat pools in my lower stomach. I slam into him in sharp, fast, staccato strokes until my climax slams into me.

"Ohhh, fuck, yes!" I cry out as I come hard.

I can't stop. I don't want to. The sounds he's making are all too delicious, and I can't help myself. I keep pushing into him, forcing my cock as deeply as he can take it, making sure he knows I own his tender little arse completely. He's my little bitch. I reach around him and touch his balls, cupping them.

"Oh, Jesus!" he moans loudly. My hand grips his cock firmly. I need him to come; I need him to make a mess of himself, to really know what a glorious little anal whore he can be for me.

I let the movement of my thrusts force his cock through the tight grasp of my hand, caressing him with every stroke in his arse, driving him forward to climax. My own orgasm is already building within me once more.

"Tell me what you are!" I demand.

He moans again, backing against me as I thrust into his arse. I drive into him hard to get his attention. "I said, TELL ME WHAT YOU ARE!" I demand again.

"Oh, God! I'm a dirty little queer," he breathes.

"Who owns your whore ass?" I ask.

"You!" he cries out, his unsteady breathing telling me just how close he is. "You! I'm your anal slut. Jesus, you fill my ass so good."

Those words are my undoing for a second time. I come harder than before, still thrusting and letting those thrusts guide his cock through my grip. He twitches, bucking against my cock and hand in equal need, and with a loud groan, he explodes in a climax. His knees give way and I pull out of him. I move to his face, his open mouth panting still, and I press my cock against his lips.

"Suck it," I demand. "Taste your ass on my cock."

His lips part more and his tongue snakes out to the underside of my big fake dick. Christ, there is nothing more delicious than this man being a filthy little slut for me, and I will never tire of putting him in his place.

Chapter Four

I lie on the hotel room bed, making myself comfortable as I wait for her to appear from the bathroom. The room has a nice, comfortable king-sized bed, and I kick off my shoes, relax, and grab the TV remote, flicking through the channels while I wait.

When she finally walks out of the bathroom, I'm enthralled with what I see. She's standing there before me with a gag in her mouth, her nipples peeping out over the top of a black and red lacy corset. They're clamped, a little silver chain linking them. She has stockings, heels, and suspenders on, and on her ankles and wrists are leather restraints.

She's got a paper luggage label hanging from one of her nipple clamps. Just looking at her like this already has me hard. I get up, move around the bed to her, and take her little label in my hand to read it.

Yours to do whatever you wish with. Plugged, clamped, gagged, and ready to use.

I free the tag from her clamp and drop it onto the bed behind me. "Plugged, huh?" I ask her, my hand running down between her legs until I find the end of a dildo pressed tightly against the entrance to her cunt, the rest of it buried inside her. I move behind her and let my other hand roam down over her ass until my fingertips discover the base of another dildo, this one firmly up her arse.

My cock throbs at the thought of her like this for me and all the possibilities that I can do with her, so willing to be mine. I take a wrist in each hand and clip the restraints together in front of her, using them to lead her over to the bed. I sit and pull her over my lap on her front, her ass up in the air, her body across my knee. I put my left hand firmly between her shoulder blades and lean into her, keeping her immobilised with my hold.

With my right hand, I stroke careful circles over her upturned arse. I rub her skin, admiring the thong she has on to keep her dildos stuffed inside her, enjoying the feeling of her body over my upright dick. I know full well that she can feel me against her side, even through my jeans.

I pull on the end of the dildo in her pussy, teasing it in and out of her just a little bit, knowing it will drive her crazy and that she will need more. After just a few strokes, she starts to squirm against my hand, wriggling on my lap. The friction she's generating against my cock is too much, and I need to put a stop to it before she takes me too far. I raise my hand and smack it down hard on her backside.

Her skin heats at the contact. Her movement ceases, and she lies on my lap, waiting for what happens next. I lift my hand again and bring it down hard on her ass. I know it's moving the dildos she's got herself plugged with. I know it's intensifying the feeling they're generating within her, but she's been a bad girl to tease me like this, looking like she does when she dresses this way. She needs to learn her lesson. I keep letting my hand connect mercilessly with her buttocks until she's starting to moan against the gag and her ass cheeks are a fiery red.

If she's moaning, she's not getting a true taste of the lesson I'm trying to give her, so I decide to give her a taste of something else instead. I slide her from my lap to the floor in front of me.

"Give me your hands," I demand. She settles on her knees and presents her wrists to me. I unclip her wrists and pull her hands behind her back. The clasps click, and her arms are secured behind her.

Her chest rises and falls in rapid movements, making my dick lurch against my underwear and jeans. She really is the hottest woman I've ever known. There isn't a part of her that I don't find sexy, and knowing what I'm about to do to her, with her so willing and wanting, is driving me fucking crazy.

I stand before her; I undo the fly on my jeans and drop them to my knees. Her eyes follow my hands as they come back to my briefs. I rub the palm of my hand against my aching cock, knowing that watching me stroke myself gets her wet.

I tug my underwear to the same level as my jeans and grab my cock firmly in my hand, tugging along my length. Fuck, it feels so good, but not as good as it's going to feel when I do what I'm about to do.

"Like what you see, do you?" I ask, and she nods at me once. I smile and let my cock drop, sticking straight out, pointing at her. I let it rub across her lips, and her tongue snakes out around the gag, needing something more, wanting to take me in. I pull the strap at the side of her mouth, and the ball pops free. She licks her lips, her eyes on my dick, and she opens up, ready for me to slide into her wet mouth.

I close my eyes at the sheer fucking bliss that washes over me when I feel her enclose around me. My fist naturally balls in her hair, and I push that little bit deeper.

"Fuck!" I hiss when her tongue laps over the underside of my cock. "Oh, fuck. You're such a good girl for me."

It would be so easy to give into the temptation of using her mouth to bring me to the climax I'm already so desperately in need of reaching. It's just her; everything about her turns me on, but when she presents herself to me like this, it's doubly so. It's taking all of my reserve to not fuck her mouth roughly. I don't want to come until I'm buried deep inside her delicious, tight cunt.

That thought proves too much, and I pull myself from between her sweet lips. I grab the ball of the gag and push it back into her mouth, fixing the straps to hold it in place.

"Get up," I demand. She eases herself from the floor in front of me with relative ease, considering her hands were still behind her back. "Bend," I order again, putting a hand on her arm to direct her to the bed.

Once her knees hit the bed, she lets me guide her body to the mattress. Standing behind her for a split second, I admire the sight of her with her ass in the air and her face in the sheets. Stroking my aching dick, I step forward, sliding my finger into her knickers and pulling them aside, revealing the end of the dildo buried in her pussy.

Taking a hold of the toy plugging her, I unsheathe it from her cunt. It glistens with her juices, and unable to resist, I pull it to my lips and lick the length of it.

"Fuck, you taste so good," I tell her, savouring her taste. A frenzy starts in me, and I just can't resist anymore. In one movement, I slide my cock deep into her, feeling the extra tightness caused by her filled asshole.

She's so soaked that I'm able to sink balls deep inside her in just one movement.

"Oh, fuck," I groan when my cock is completely enshrouded in her warmth. My hands grip her hips, and driven by a deep need, I begin a rhythm of thrusts which pull me almost completely free of her before driving hard back inside.

Moaning vibrates through the bed, and I pick up the pace of my thrusts. I've allowed myself to get too worked up and now I need the release. I can't control the need to fuck her; I buck my hips against her as my fingers dig firmly into her skin.

"I'm going to come inside you," I warn her. "I'm going to fill you. I need to know that you're full of my cum."

My climax roars through me the second her pussy tightens around my cock as she is engulfed in her own orgasm. I use it to drive deep into her one last time.

I savour the pulses of her pussy as they milk the last of my cum from my cock before pulling out of her and collapsing on the bed beside her. I unclip her hands and pull her in against me. She pulls the gag from her mouth and moulds her body into my side.

"Don't remove anything," I whisper against the top of her head. "I'm not finished with you yet."

A contented sigh blows across my chest, and I hold her tight and nod off until I'm ready for round two.

Chapter Five

My heart is pounding in my chest as we walk into the hotel room. We had been talking about it for months now, and finally, we found someone we wanted to help us out. He's a nice guy, funny with a touch of cheeky, which put me completely at ease with him. He's into the same field of work as you, so you and he have been talking shop and getting on like a house on fire. Of course, this time it's going to be different.

Richie leads me towards the bed, leaving you behind to watch. He yanks me tight against him, his hands on my neck, and pulls me hard against him, his mouth enveloping mine, his tongue almost instantly probing my mouth. He presses hard against me in the kind of kiss that makes me feel like he just can't get enough of me or get me close enough. It's loaded with that raw, 'got to have you' sensation. I find it invigorating. Especially knowing you're there watching it all happen.

You move towards us and mould your body against my back, and your hands find my hips. Your length presses at my arse; you're already hard and all he's done is kiss me.

Your lips find my neck, and he stops kissing me to watch what you're doing. When you lift your head to look at him, I see that flash in both your eyes. You both lean over my shoulder, utilising the fact that I'm shorter than you to move in and kiss each other. I watch, wedged between you, feeling you both grind against me as you let your tongues explore each other's mouths. My pussy is already soaked from finding myself smack in the middle of the sexiest thing I've ever seen. One delicious hot red-blooded male getting off on another.

I try to slip away from between the two of you, intent on getting a better view of what's happening, and instead, you grab me around the waist and pull me back against you both. Richie's hands go for mine, and he guides me over his cock and yours, pressing my palm against you both, telling me what he wants from me while never breaking his physical connection to you.

You both roll your hips against my hand as I press hard against you. I feel how hard you both are, how turned on and needy you're both getting as you push yourselves against my hands. I drop my hand from his cock, and I move to free yours, undoing your jeans and moving them just enough to let your cock free. I then do the same with Richie's. When you're both exposed to me, I can't help but bend between you and lick along the heads of both your dicks.

You and Richie gasp, breaking your kiss and staring down at me and what I'm doing. I gaze up at you both, taking one of you into my wet mouth before swapping sides and taking in the other. I alternate between your delicious cocks, lapping at each of you, sucking on you both. I look up at you and see you watching me while I suck on Richie, and I know that look only too well.

"Do you want to taste him?" I ask you before I sink my mouth back over you again. You moan as I do.

"Oh, fuck, yes," you breathe, and Richie smirks at your answer.

Richie takes a step back from us. He pulls his t-shirt over his head, revealing his lean torso and speckling of manly body hair. His jeans and boxers disappear too, and he stands there in all his full glory. I glance at you as your eyes feast on him all over. I smirk and catch your eye.

"I think you're just a little bit overdressed now, my love," I tease, and you don't hesitate in taking off your t-shirt and jeans and standing in front of us both naked.

My eyes feast on you, naked, broad-shouldered, and all that delicious chest hair I can't keep my hands off.

"Get on your knees," I demand.

Your hands instinctively cover your cock while you sink to the floor. I get up and move behind Richie, pushing him closer to you until he's standing right in front of you. I reach around him and wrap my hand around his cock, pumping him a few times, keeping my eyes fixed on you as I do.

"Open your mouth," I tell you.

You do, and I push him one step closer to you, his cock just in front of your face. I move to his side, reach out, grab you by the back of the head, and shove your face and waiting open mouth over Richie's cock. I set the speed and movement of you both together, him thrusting and you pushing your mouth against him to take him even deeper. Once your hands reach for his thighs to pull him against you, I let you both go and bend to whisper loudly in your ear.

"You love sucking a real cock, don't you, my little queer?" I ask.

You moan, and Richie's eyes roll back in his head at the

sensation of you murmuring around his cock. I run my hands over his body, grazing over his nipples as I do. Once utterly satisfied with the floor show, I step back and rest myself on the bottom of the bed to watch.

Richie's hand takes hold of the back of your head. He's intently watching his cock slip in and out past your lips. You're looking up at him, focused on taking all of him into your mouth. I'm watching, lying back on the bed, running my hands over my clothing. I'm so utterly turned on by what I'm seeing. My hot alpha man with this younger guy, doing things that, until now, he has only dreamed of doing.

My hand grazes the inside of my thigh as I watch, transfixed at the glorious sight of you being face fucked for the first time by another man. I slip my hand into the waistband of my lacy knickers, and I spread myself wide, needing to take care of myself while you too skilfully take care of Richie. One stroke of my fingers over my cunt confirms what I already knew; I am utterly soaked, turned on so much by what I'm experiencing right now.

Richie watches me run my fingertips over my clit, soft moans falling from my lips. He watches me watching him, and I know it's only adding to his arousal. His grip tightens at the back of your neck, his breathing a little erratic as he watches me playing with myself. I gaze at you as you look at what I'm doing too. I hear your moan, and when I do, Richie's head drops back and he's lodging himself at the back of your throat. He groans, and I watch you gag. My own climax rises in my groin. I know he's pumping your mouth full of his hot cum, and you're loving every minute while I play with my pussy for you both.

He steps back and lets his semi-erect cock slide from between your lips, and your eyes are still focused on me as he sits down in the armchair in the corner of the room. I know the look on your face, and I watch as you rise from the floor and move towards me. I move back on the bed, knowing you're coming for me like I'm prey. You follow me over the bed, lining yourself up between my legs. Your body covers mine and you lean down and kiss me, hard and hungry. The taste of Richie's cum is still all over your tongue and you roll it over mine.

You sit up on your knees and look down at me. You spread my legs wider and tug the crotch of my knickers to the side, waiting for nothing as you push your cock inside me in one stroke.

"Did you enjoy sucking a real cock?" I ask with a smile.

"I did," you tell me.

I gasp as you press your cock into the deepest parts of me with the next thrust. "And did you enjoy drinking his cum, my little slut?"

"Oh, fuck, yes," you say with a roll of your hips.

You pick up the pace and mix things up with a roll of your hips and hard, deep thrusts on every stroke. You tease me to orgasm again and again, while Richie watches. I look at him by the time I'm coming back down from my third climax and notice he's hard again, stroking his cock as he surveys the show we're putting on.

The thrill of having a witness to our fucking washes over me, and I can't help but come even harder the next time. He stands when I do, moving over towards the bed, his cock in his hand, jerking his length as he disappears behind you. I hear him flick the lid on a bottle of lube as he reappears in my line of sight, directly behind you.

"Wait," he tells you, with a hand on your back as you have yourself deep in my wet pussy. He manoeuvres behind you, and your cock twitches inside me when the head of his cock rubs against your asshole. This is what you've been waiting for, to have your ass fucked hard by a real cock that can leave a hot load deep inside you.

I wrap my legs around your thighs and pull your legs apart slightly, holding you tight against me, yet giving Richie more access to your slutty little arsehole. I know the second he has penetrated you because your whole body tenses for an instant and then relaxes. I wait, letting Richie work his way deep into your ass before he starts thrusting against you. You both start to move, setting a rhythm that suits you. You pull back from my pussy and push back on him, then sink back into me hard, as I'm pounded with the force of two driving forward.

You set a harsh pace with each other. Driving hard against each other and taking me along for the ride with you. I climax over and over as Richie fucks your ass hard, and you fuck my cunt as deeply as you can.

"Oh, God! Tell him where you want his cum, you fucking slut," I demand of you.

You moan and grind harder against me.

"Tell me," Richie commands.

"Fuck!" you pant. "Up my ass. Ohh, fuck! Come up my gay ass." You sigh on a moan.

Richie's pace picks up again, his hands grabbing your hips. "I'm going to fill your arse, you little bitch. Fucking take it," he growls. His words make me climax, and with him unloading his cum in your ass and me clenching your cock and soaking it more, you let go, roaring as your whole body jerks, and you flood my pussy with your cum.

He slips from your ass and moves off the bed, positioning himself near your face. "Suck it," he tells you, and you run your mouth hungrily over his cock. Once satisfied with your clean-up job, he encourages you to move back and out of my cunt. He dips his head as you do, and you hiss as he licks my juices from your cock.

Richie drops himself down on the bed beside me. You drop on the other side, and the three of us lie there, caressing each other lovingly as we all come down from our powerful climaxes. Each of you rests a head on one of my breasts, and I kiss the top of your heads.

"What a perfect little pair of filthy little queers you are," I tease. I can't wait to see what the rest of the evening holds for us all.

Chapter Six

When she finally gets home, I need to be inside her immediately. Hell, I have since before she left for work this morning, when I pulled her knickers aside, slid into her, and pumped her full of my cum.

I wanted her to smell me on her pussy all day. I wanted her to have a constant reminder of where I had been and what I had done. I needed to have her thinking of me as much as I'd be thinking of her at work, in that dress she knows drives me crazy. She's mine, and I like to keep reminding her of it. I like to keep marking my territory, claiming her with cum.

I move towards her after she closes the door. She smiles at me, and I wrap my arms around her and hug her tight against me, needing her close. I lean in and place my lips against her neck, softly at first. Then, I can't help myself. She presses against me, and I draw her skin harder against my mouth with a suck. I know it's going to mark her, but I really can't resist it.

Her head falls back, and a moan escapes her lips. It's all I need to tip me over. I grab at the skirt of her dress, tugging it up enough for me to dip my hand below the hem. My hand runs along her stocking-covered thigh as my mouth moves back to hers before I find the edge of her lacy knickers and waste no time in plunging a finger deep into her cunt. She's so fucking wet, as I knew she would be.

"That's my good girl," I purr against her lips, and I work a second finger deep into her, starting a steady thrust with my hand. "Always so fucking wet and ready for me, aren't you?"

A moan is her only reply, and the slight blush on her cheeks tells me how right I am, and how much she's enjoying being called a good girl. I slip a third finger against the other two, and I let my thumb roll over her clit as she grinds against the stroke of my hand. She's getting so close to coming for me already.

"Mmm, that's my good girl. You want to come, don't you?" I ask.

"Oh, fuck, yes!" she tells me, her breathing rapid and her heart pounding.

There are two ways I can play this. I can either give her the orgasm she so desperately craves already, or I could pull my hand out of her pussy now and lick my fingers as I walk away. But she gives me that look, the one I know too well, and I know it will only end one way. With her quaking around my fingers as her juices coat my hand.

I rub her clit a little bit faster, with a touch more pressure, as I push my fingers as deeply as she can take them. I look at her, catching her gaze, making sure she can't look away, and I say what she needs to hear. "Come for me."

She coats my fingers and hand in the seconds after I've said it. I'm so fucking hard for her; I press myself against her as she cries out against me. "Such a good fucking girl." I smile and press my lips on hers, swallowing her moans of satisfaction.

When I pull my fingers from inside her, she shakes against me at their loss, but I already have other ideas of what will happen next. I step back from her, and one by one, I take each of my fingers and suck her from them. I fucking love how she tastes, and I will definitely be feasting on her afterwards. For now, I have a cock that's painfully rubbing against my underwear and jeans, and I know just the place for it.

I push her shoulder, and she needs no further encouragement or instruction. Her knees bend and she sinks to the floor, looking up at me expectantly. I undo my jeans and gaze at her.

"You know what I want," I tell her. And she does.

She takes my jeans and pulls them to my knees, her hands running over my skin, caressing my thighs as she returns to my briefs. She stares up with eyes filled with lust and satisfaction and runs her palm firmly over my swollen length.

"Fuck," I groan, putting both hands on the wall behind her, far above her head, bracing myself for what she's about to do.

Her hands rub again over my cock, and I glare at her, silently telling her not to try that again; I won't be able to take her teasing me. She knows me well enough to pull my briefs down to meet my jeans and let my dick spring out in front of her. She looks at it, licking her lips like it's a meal she's been dying for all day, then closes her eyes as she takes me into her warm, wet mouth.

Fuck, she really is too much. I rest my head on the wall in front of me, my eyes closed, and just enjoy every sensation that's washing over me. The feel of her tongue on the bottom side of my dick. The wetness of her saliva as she spreads it over me. The strength of her suck when she pulls me deep into her sweet little mouth.

Just as I lose myself in that feeling, her hands arrive on my outer thighs. She shifts below me, getting comfortable as she grabs my ass and pulls me deeper into her. The head of my cock hits her gag reflex. I open my eyes and look down to find her looking up at me. Her eyes start to water as she fights the natural urge to expel what's in her throat.

I'm about to pull back from her just a little when I feel her finger against my asshole. "Oh, fuck. That's my good girl," I tell her, pulling back out of her mouth just enough to let her get her breath before she pushes her finger partway into my ass. I can't help but thrust forward. Every movement I make in her mouth, she makes with her finger in my ass, and I know if she keeps that up, she'll be swallowing the load I've been saving for her all day. But that's not where I want it to go. I enjoy the feeling of her finger getting deeper and deeper up my arse as I push my cock repeatedly against the back of her throat.

She looks sexy as hell when I look down on her and see her eyes wet from taking me deep and encouraging me to fuck her gorgeous face. The need to be buried deep in her pussy is more than I can bear when I look at how amazing my dick looks sinking into her sweet mouth.

I force myself to pull my cock from between her lips, and she lets me, her finger slipping from my ass. She repeats my actions and slides her finger between her lips and licks it, tasting me. I heave my jeans and briefs from half-mast, then grab her wrists and pull her to her feet, guiding her through the house until we reach the bedroom.

"Hands and knees," I demand as she looks over her shoulder at me. She lifts the hem of her dress so she doesn't kneel on it and crawls onto the bed, kneeling just as I asked her to. This time the jeans and briefs come off, along with my t-shirt, soon standing behind her completely naked. Joining her on the bed from behind, letting my hands stroke her thighs up under her dress lifting it completely, leaving her sexy ass exposed to me.

I have teased myself as well as her, and I can't wait any longer than I need to. As much as I love the sight of her naked and spread for me, that would just take too fucking long. I find the crotch of her knickers, pull them to the side, and guide my cock into her soaked slit.

I slide into her in one stroke, balls deep in her tight little pussy. I know by how she clenches me when I'm as deep as I can be that she's felt the stretch she tells me is so delicious. I pull back, watching my cock move out of her, slick with her juices before I delight in the sight of it sliding all the way back inside her. Fuck, I could watch that for hours. There is no sight more gorgeous to me than that of her beautiful pussy taking all of my bare cock, just like it was made for that very activity. However, hours of this would have my balls blue enough to drop off.

I push against her and she pushes back on me; looking to feel me just that little bit deeper. My girl is always so greedy for what I have to give her. I hold on to her hips as I pump into her hard and fast. She clamps down around me, and I know another orgasm is about to rip through her. She cries out and clenches down on my cock so hard I stop moving, buried as deep as I can be, and enjoy the waves of climax as they flood around my dick and grip me hard.

When I feel her relax, I pick up the pace, thrusting deep and hard, knowing she'll come again pretty soon. I need her to; every time she does it pushes me closer to my own peak. I thrust and thrust, stopping only as a few more of her orgasms grip my cock, until she pushes me past the point where I could stop. I feel it starting in my balls, and I know I'm going to fill her with cum.

"Oh, fuck. I'm going to come. Where do you want it?" I pant.

A groan rumbles through her and she pushes back on me again. "Oh, God. You'd better flood my cunt. I need it... oh, God!" she begs. "Give me your cum!"

Her pussy tightens again as she speaks those words, but I can't think or hold back any longer. I slam deep inside her as she says it and unload into her, flooding her just as she asked me to.

I pull her onto her side with me, still hard enough to remain buried deep inside her as I do. I wrap my arms around her as we both come back down to earth from the heavens above. I hold her tight against me, utterly content that her sweet little cunt is full of me and my cum. I will savour its taste and smell it up close when she's sitting on my face, but for now, I'm very pleased to leave some of myself deep inside her.

* * *

Enjoy this? Why not read the next in the series - Owned

The One-Handed Reads Series is made to do exactly what you might think!

Master Owen knows what he wants.

I need to give him what he wants. I had never been submissive until him. The more Owen gives me glimpses into his world, the more and more intrigued I am.

He led me down the path to submission, like the white rabbit leading Alice into Wonderland. Now, I am hooked, addicted to the pleasure that only he can generate in me.

I am his. I am OWNED.

About the Author

Dee Lish is an Irish author who loves to indulge her imagination with some filthy stories. She's been publishing under other pen names since 2014, but in 2023 returned to her erotic roots.

She likes to spend what little spare time she has binge watching her favourite shows, reading, and making messes and memories with her two children.

You can follow her on social media, or join her newsletter for all the latest naughtiness!

Also by Dee Lish

Succumb to Me Series

The Mistress

The Ponygirl

The Handled

The Punished

The Corrupted

The Student

One Handed Reads Series

Teased

Owned

Seduced

Tempted

Desired

Unexpected

* * *

Dee Lish also writes romance as Leighann Duncan

www.authorleighannduncan.co.uk